GL

The Mind

a novel

THE MIND by Gloria Foster
Published by Creation House
A Charisma Media Company
600 Rinehart Road
Lake Mary, Florida 32746
www.charismamedia.com

Cover design by Linda Gillotti

Visit the author's website: www.gloriafoster.com

Library of Congress Control Number: 2017912621
International Standard Book Number:
978-1-62999-225-9
E-book International Standard Book Number:
978-1-62999-226-6

First edition

17 18 19 20 21 — 987654321
Printed in the United States of America

This novel is dedicated to
Gabrielle, my daughter, and Bobby,
my father, whose memories I cherish.

HALLUCINATION

*Creating
messages
into
mind,
inconveniently
releasing
fear
beyond
comprehension.*

Contents

Guide

IT WAS A bright, clear day in the middle of June that I found myself driving with no car in sight on a usually packed highway, not a cloud in the sky. I turned up the volume on my radio to block out the voices. I have always had to have the radio on because sometimes the voices get scary. Yet, I must admit that sometimes they help me out. This one particular voice continues to be there just when I need the answers to the questions in my life.

I can't believe how beautiful this day is. The color blue has many hues, and it always seems as though the color of the sky varies. Today is a bright, oh-so-beautiful blue that I never could find in a crayon box.

I felt the vibration of my cell phone in the pocket of my white knit jersey, and my assumption was accurate that it was Jonathan. *I wonder what Jonathan wants.*

"Hi, Jonathan."

"Where are you?"

"On Stone City Highway headed towards town to check up on a few matters."

"Just checking up on you," he said. "How have you been? Did you get to decide where we're going to have dinner this evening?"

"I think we could dine in," I answered.

"Come on. You haven't been out in a while."

"I'm out now, Jonathan."

"You think?"

1

"I'll give you a call when I come up with where we're going," he said.

"OK, Jonathan."

Back to the radio, I thought. I upped the volume. Most of the songs on 98.7 AM don't have any words to them. No lyrics.

The only time I'll hear a live voice is when the radio announcer comes on between the music. It's so peaceful listening to the music.

I don't know what Jonathan is going to come up with for tonight. Who knows, I might be headed back towards town again this evening.

My last turn, I thought as I turned left into the parking garage. I'm going to check on the trip to San Jose. Out of all places, they want to reunite in San Jose.

I reached for my handbag. I opened the car door. After stepping out onto the pavement, I straightened my white cotton dress. This was where I usually parked when I came to town because of familiarity. *Even when my parents rode into town, my father used to park in this same location*, I thought. *It used to be a parking lot.*

I placed the caramel colored leather strap of my handbag onto my shoulder and made it out of the garage to the street, taking in the soothing heat from the sun, which shone brightly. As I was walking, I reached into the outer pocket of my handbag and pulled out my chocolate-brown framed sunglasses that had a very dark brown tint. *That's better. My eyes are at ease. Thank you, God*, I thought.

It was always busy in town. *The sidewalk is packed on both sides of the street. Let's see. I should be close. Here it is—1168 Chipperdau Road.*

As I entered the building I noticed a strange darkness. How could it be this dim and dreary in a travel agency?

"How may I help you?" the receptionist asked. She was a stout lady with oval-shaped eyes and dark, brunette hair. She had a round face. When she spoke, her voice resounded and brought life to the dull room.

"I'm here to inquire about airfare and accommodations to San Jose during the second week of September," I replied.

"If you would have a seat, someone will be with you shortly."

I couldn't have helped but notice the square-shaped gray sofa when I had entered the room. The sofa was a shade lighter than the walls in the place. I turned around, walked back to the entranceway, and sat down onto a very comfortable couch that was very much lighter than my charcoal gray car seat.

"Ma'am, I forgot to ask your name," the receptionist asked me from where she was seated. She had a different pitch to her voice than before. *How could her voice have changed?* I thought to myself.

"Sheila," I responded. "My name is Sheila Leclaire."

"Will you be doing business with us today, ma'am?"

"More than likely," I answered.

Then I heard a loud voice in my ear.

» *Stop talking to her!* «

"Someone will be with you shortly ma'am," stated the receptionist.

OK, I thought. *I'm going to sit here really still until my mind gets back to normal.* When I hear voices, I can't think. The voices block out everything else in my mind until I normalize and come back to reality.

Maybe I should go back to the car to turn on the radio or just go back home, I thought. What a horrible, horrible feeling.

"Ms. Leclaire?"

I looked up, and a very tall gentleman with darkish brown hair and a solemn, small, rectangular-shaped face had gotten very close to the couch where I was seated without me recognizing his presence. He was standing very close in front of me. I steadily lifted my head up rather high, viewing his tall, slender appearance. He had a very blank expression to his face.

"What brings you here today?" he asked.

"I'm here to secure a trip to San Jose in September," I answered. "The second week in September."

He held out his arm for me to shake his hand. *His hand is rather cold,* I thought as he clasped his hand to mine.

"Follow me," he stated and turned slowly.

I arose from the couch, and we walked past the receptionist, who was methodically typing and looking into her computer screen. I continued walking, following the gentleman through an acorn-colored door and down the hallway.

"Charles Norbin is my name, and I'll be helping you out," he stated as we walked down the narrow hallway until we reached his office.

"Sit down please," he said.

He was seated with his arms on his desk, his hands in a round, opened-fist position. He spoke gently and rhythmically. He took all my information and went over flight information and hotel accommodations for my trip reuniting me and three of my best friends from high school. Those three girls and I were all quite different and had different personalities, but one of the things we had in common was our involvement in one of the community organizations for disadvantaged youngsters in Washington, DC. We all lived in Sommerville, Virginia, an affluent city right outside of DC, and it brought us great joy to be able to help mold the future of our peers who were not given the same opportunities at that point in their lives as we were.

» *Stop thinking!* «

The voice interrupted my thinking.

"Ms. Leclaire?"

I froze as Charles Norbin tried to get my attention.

"Ms. Leclaire," he stated. "Ms. Albright says she'll mail your reservation package in a few days."

"Yes?" I said.

"Thank you," I answered.

"Here is your itinerary," he said.

"You looked like you were somewhere else, ma'am," stated the receptionist as she handed me the sheet of paper. I hadn't noticed she had entered the room.

"Ms. Leclaire, everything here is finished," she said. "So, you'll pay on your way out."

I rose from my seat. "Thank you."

I then heard a very scary voice:

» *Shut up!* «

The receptionist rushed around to my side. "Follow me," she said.

I walked behind her, continuing through the hallway and acorn-colored door until I reached her desk.

"If you don't receive the package Mr. Norbin was referring to, call me back," she said. "Mail is iffy here."

"All right," I stated as I handed her a check.

When I reached the fresh air and sunlight I began to feel somewhat better, although I was puzzled and frightened at the magnitude and intensity of the voices. I was totally interrupted by the voices. The voice scared and shocked me. It's the same feeling that the heart has when someone jumps out in front of them from nowhere. But, unlike this real example of being frightened, there is no reality to explain a hallucination, so this total loss of control as well as the unexpected nature of the voices was horrific.

As I reached my car, I noticed a few clouds had appeared out of nowhere. They were moving fast to form a mostly grayish white sky as I gazed upward when I had my automobile key in the keyhole of my darkish green Dodge.

As I backed out of the parking lot, there were more cars on the street than people walking on the sidewalk. I must've been in Venture Sales longer than I thought. As I flipped the switch on my radio dial, it started to drizzle on my windshield. I turned the switch to increase the speed of my wipers as the rainfall increased.

I then heard another voice say,

» *Careful driving.* «

Now that was a normal one.

Comfort

As I entered the front door of my condominium, I reached down to pick up *The Daily Gazette.* I opened the front door, and as I placed every item I was holding on the pine entrance table, my telephone rang.

I entered my living room, picked up the phone, and struck a match to light my orange-and-nutmeg spiced candle.

"Hello, Jonathan," I said. "I made the arrangements for travel in early fall."

"Good," he said. "How about eight thirty?"

"Wonderful."

"Well, we're going to be out and about for a while this evening, and Marquise Davis is playing tonight at The Checker Joint. We can't miss that band, lady love."

"Oh, Jonathan, you continue to be as charming as ever."

"As charming as ever, my dear," he replied. "All right, it is going to be a long doozy of a night with you, my friend. Pick up at six thirty sharp."

"Six thirty sharp it is."

"What would I do without you!" we both stated in unison, as we usually did.

"Later, Girl Sheila," he said.

I put the phone on my wall hook and started to heat up some water in my tea kettle. Tea was something I definitely could not live without. I had placed a bag of mild black and a dash of allspice into my round cup

7

as the kettle started to whiz. I added a teaspoon of honey and stirred as I poured the just-right hot water over the bag.

I stood sipping my tea as I pondered the events of the day. It was always good to hear from Jonathan. *Maybe in the future I will share with Jonathan what is going on in this mind of mine.*

As I sipped on the remainder of my tea, which always seemed to be sweeter during the last drop, I decided a warm bath was in order.

I climbed the stairs to the second level of my condominium, walked down the hallway, and entered my bedroom. It was usually very peaceful in my bedroom, but today it felt kind of eerie. *Let me get a view of outside*, I thought as I cracked my window and heard birds chirping. They had formed a nest in one of the tall oak trees that lined the boulevards in my neighborhood. I unbuttoned my cotton dress from top to bottom and slipped on my robe. I turned on my stereo on the nightstand beside my bed.

After entering the adjacent bathroom, I turned on the hot water first until it had reached the highest possible temperature and slowly adjusted the temperature by turning the cold water knob until it had reached the perfect temperature. I reached for my strawberry-vanilla bubble bath and poured a capful under the water, thereby forming a host of bubbles. I adjusted my radio to the local jazz station. I disrobed and slipped into my bubble-filled tub.

My back was situated adjacent to the tub, and I had gotten comfortable when I heard a voice.

» *Everything all right?* «

I continued to soak and tune into the rhythm of the music, imagining each instrument distinctly to remain focused. Then the voices got stronger.

» *La-la-la-la-la. Can't get away. La-la-la-la-la.* «

The voices continued over the instruments, causing interference with my jazz and the peace and tranquility I had established, or at least tried to establish, in my own domain. I raised my hands through the bubbles, taking my two forefingers and placing them over my ears in an attempt to block out all sound.

» *Stop!* «

Yet, all I heard was the voice with fading jazz. I hurriedly towel dried.

» *Can't get away.* «

I set my alarm to 5:30 pm while I fell off to sleep with jazz music playing. I faded into my dream of my mother and father.

"Everything is going to be all right Mr. Leclaire," a gentleman stated. "Did you make a statement to the police?"

"Yes, I did when we arrived."

"She was left for dead out there by the river."

"We have resuscitated her, and she is going to be just fine."

"If I get my hands on the—"

"William, the police are handling the situation. Out of all that has happened we cannot find ourselves turned away from the needs of Sheila."

"Millie! I have a daughter that almost died too! They are not going to get away with almost beating her to death."

Jonathan

Jonathan had arrived exactly on time as usual.

"Sheila, have I ever stood you up or been late to pick you up in all these years?" Jonathan asked.

"No," I answered. "You're always on time."

"That's true, Sheila," he said. "We've been friends quite a while, and I know everything about you."

"You only know what I choose to let you know, Jonathan Stevenson."

"What's my favorite food?" I asked.

"Chop suey."

"Then why are we not doing Chinese?"

"We can," he said.

"What's my favorite color, Mr. Jonathan? You think you know everything about Sheila."

"Sweet potato orange."

"You remember I like that color?"

"Yea."

"Good," I said.

"We don't know anything about each other yet," I teased.

"But that is a fantastic arrangement," I mused as we arrived out in front of The Checker Joint. It was jammed packed for a Thursday evening.

Jonathan switched off the ignition and opened up his car door. He was wearing a white short-sleeved knit shirt with dark navy tailored pants. He exited the car quickly and before I knew it had gotten around the car to open my door.

Turning, I put one leg out of the car. I was wearing sheer light hose with two-inch front-strapped heels in cream. There were rhinestones in the middle of each shoe with three straps angling out of each side of the shiny, clear rhinestones. I was wearing a ruffled-bottom, white short skirt with a matching white blouse ruffled at the arms, neckline, and hem. It had polka dots in pale pink and off-white.

I had on my favorite iridescent white bracelet, diamond-studded earrings, and marquise diamond ring.

As I exited Jonathan's car and stood up, my long ponytail bounced from side to side as the ruffles on my clothing swayed into their proper place.

Jonathan closed the door of his white Corvette with black leather interior and took my right hand. My ponytail bounced as we walked somewhat briskly toward the dinner club.

There were several people standing outside of The Checker Joint conversating. One man with his date was smoking.

As we moved closer to the restaurant I noticed the entryway off to the side that consisted of dark, reddish brown and gray stones. The landscaping was beyond belief with various sized evergreens, tropicals, and large flowering bushes in different shades of pink. Jonathan reached for the two-bar handle and opened the wide, heavy, wooden, dark-charcoal gray door with a centered window. It had thick square grids through which I could see light and the movement of the people in The Checker Joint.

As we walked through the entryway, I smelled the aroma of the food on the grills instantaneously.

There was no one in line at the hostess's counter. As we proceeded toward her, she smiled a wide smile with pearly white, shiny teeth, and shiny gloss covered her lips perfectly. She had a square-shaped face. Her brunette, shoulder-length hair was feathered to perfection. She had on a white blouse, black dress pants, and shiny silver strapped high heels. Her diamond necklace and wedding ring took in light surrounding the booth where she was seated.

Jonathan and I ended up at a table right away, and as soon as we were seated a gentleman announced that Marquise Davis's band was about to start playing.

As I peered over to the area where the band had started playing, I noticed the beauty of The Checker Joint. There was water flowing over the stones and flowers and greenery arranged as a backdrop behind the musicians. The table where Jonathan and I were seated was at ground level with about fifty tables with floor plants in the area. The flooring was maroon carpeting and dark pine wood. There were two levels to the right of us with tables that had a view of the band. Ahead of where we were seated was one raised level with windows with a view of the pier. The moonlight and stars were visible even from the ground floor.

While I noted the star-filled sky, the band softly played, and our waiter arrived and inquired if we were ready to order.

I stated my order, and I noticed that, as usual, everyone at The Checker Joint gave full attention to the band playing.

"I'll have the lobster stir fry, artichokes, and baked potato."

Jonathan ordered filet mignon, vegetable medley with cauliflower, carrots, and baby onions, and rice pilaf.

"The band is getting down tonight," stated Jonathan.

"Yes, they are!"

» *You don't know.* «

The sound of those words caught me off guard, and a chill ran through me. The voice was different than the other ones that I had heard earlier today and unlike any in the past. It sounded as if it were a drunk man wobbling his slow words—slowly toothing and tongueing his consonants and echoing his vowels.

The result of the auditory verbiage left me feeling stalked and fearful, almost like the fear one experiences when an abusive person raises their hand to strike.

"Something wrong, Sheila?" stated Jonathan.

My expression must have changed when I had heard that bone-chilling voice. I was usually good at hiding my inner feelings when I heard disturbing voices. I managed to recoup my appearance as I answered him.

"I just thought I heard something," I stated.

"You heard something?"

"Yes, ever since I can remember, I have heard these strange voices," I said as I looked around the dinner club to see who noticed me.

"Nobody is listening to us, Sheila," he said. "They're all tuned into the band, as usual."

"Ever since I can remember—even when I was younger; as a matter of fact, as far back as my memory goes—I have always heard strange things."

"Can you explain yourself, Sheila?"

"Do you ever hear something inside of your head?" I questioned.

"Like what?" he asked.

"Like a voice."

"Do you mean hear myself when I talk or hear other people when they speak?"

"No, Jonathan. Do you ever—? I hear voices when no one is talking if I am around other people and when I am alone, Jonathan."

"Well, what do you hear?"

"I hear a person talking inside my head. The voice comes out of nowhere and happens whenever. The person says different things, and it is not my voice or consistent with my own thoughts. But it is mostly words," I said. "Mostly mean words out of nowhere. They are very frightening sometimes."

"Sheila, this has been going on as long as you can remember?" he asked.

"Yes, off and on, beginning when I was a child."

"Sheila, relax," he said. "Let me think about what you have told me tonight."

"All right?" he asked.

"All right, Jonathan," I answered.

The waiter returned with our orders and placed them on the bright white tablecloth. I had ordered hot black tea with a twist of lemon. Jonathan asked for another ice water.

"Sheila, you don't drink anymore, right?" he asked.

"Jonathan, I have not drank in several months."

"I heard it makes it worse," Jonathan said.

"Worse?"

"The voices," he said. "You're hearing voices. That's what it sounds like."

"It is such a problem! Jonathan, it wrecks my whole life. A voice enters into my mind and scares the heck out of me. A voice enters into my mind and makes me think about something sad because the voices can be so mean, and I don't know how to stop them. For instance, we are supposed to be having a nice evening out, and this voice comes out of nowhere and says, '*You don't know!*'"

"Male or female?" Jonathan asked.

"Male."

"What kind of voice or tone?"

"A man's harsh, evil voice."

"Say it like he said it."

I gruffed out the blurry, deep echoing voice, *"You don't know!"* I noticed the shock on Jonathan's face in hearing the unfamiliar sounds of my intonation.

"That is scary, Sheila," he said. "To tell you the truth, I'd be scared too if that voice came out of nowhere. Did you ever know anyone who had a voice like that?"

"No, Jonathan."

"You might not know if you did."

"What do you mean?" I asked.

"Can you place a picture with the voice?"

"No."

"I am going to have to think about this Sheila," he said. "Something is very awkward about what you have told me here tonight. Stay calm, Sheila. Do you want some more tea?"

"Yes."

Jonathan and I finished eating dinner and stayed at The Checker Joint until 11:30 pm. After Jonathan had driven me home, departed, and was headed home, I stood in my entryway with my back against my white wooden door reminiscing about the evening with Jonathan and wondering if I should have explained to him what was going on in my mind.

Void

» **YOU DON'T REMEMBER** *anything!* «
I heard as I reached the top of the short stairway to the second floor of my condominium. I decided to try to drown the voices out of my mind and proceeded down the stairs to my kitchen. I reached toward the cabinet next to my lighted cabinet with the crisscrossed door and after opening it reached far back and grabbed an unopened bottle of whiskey.

"Jonathan did not have any indication as to how to stop these voices tonight," I said aloud. "I need a temporary fix because I will not be able to see a doctor tonight."

I scooped four cubes of ice into the bottom of my heavy, clear, bumpy cocktail glass. I poured whisky and sipped glass after glass after glass until my grandfather clock struck three o'clock in the morning. I hadn't turned on the music again, determining that was a preventive cure to the events of the prior evening. I had finished one-half of the entire bottle, and the alcohol vapor continued to rise from inside my inner organs through my throat and into my nostrils. I decided to arise and continue upstairs. With my feet planted into my shag carpet, I slowly stood upward. In arising, it seemed as if the Earth's axis had changed, because my surroundings slowly spun.

» *Die!* «

Oh my gosh! All I needed was for the voices to return.
I fell to my side and crawled to the bottom of the stairs.

» *You ain't worth anything! Die!* «

I grabbed the shag fibers of the carpet as the room spinning caused me to rock unsteadily each way. I climbed the stairs on my hands and knees, sobbing and crawling until I reached my frigid bathroom floor.

» *Die! Die! Die!* «

The voice got louder and faster as a mixture of bitter medicinal and alcohol remnants filled my mouth, becoming my only reality—not sight, not sound, and not memory.

Down

"**H**I, THIS IS Sheila Leclaire. Just leave your number at the beep please."

"Girl Sheila, pick up at 9:30 a.m. for breakfast," stated Jonathan. "On my way."

Jonathan Stevenson arrived at the home of Sheila Leclaire at 9:30 a.m. sharp and proceeded to her front entry. He rapped on the door a couple of times, and when no one answered, he proceeded to get the door key hidden under a flower planter on Sheila's front porch, as he usually did when she didn't answer the door because she was in the shower when he arrived.

"Sheila," he yelled. "It's Johnny! I'm downstairs. I'm going to grab some water."

"Has she been drinking?" Jonathan questioned as he quickly noticed the half-empty bottle of whiskey that was out of place in an ordinarily picture-perfect kitchen. Sheila always had everything in place.

"Why would she choose to start back drinking? We had just talked about not drinking last night."

Jonathan wondered if she was all right since she didn't answer the phone earlier. He rushed upstairs and almost tripped when, as he turned left toward her bedroom, he noticed Sheila's legs visible from the hall bathroom doorway. He pulled his cell phone from the inside of his blazer pocket and called 9-1-1. He peered over into the bathroom, kneeling toward her body.

"Sheila!"

"Wake up, Sheila!"

She must have passed out, he thought. He placed his finger on her neck as well as her arm and felt a slight pulse.

"Oh my God! Sheila," he cried. "My Sheila. How could I have left you alone last night, dear Sheila?"

Jonathan wondered how long she was lying here in the doorway. He hoped and prayed that Sheila would awaken as the ambulance arrived. They placed Sheila on a stretcher and took her out of the house. Jonathan dashed into his Corvette and raced to St. Matthew Hospital.

Swing

I OPENED MY EYES as I drifted back to reality and swung over the white sheet and light blue colored blanket. As I reached for the IV cord with my left hand, Jonathan caught my hand in midair with placement as if we both were each half praying.

"Why am I in the hospital, Jonathan?" I asked as I looked up.

"You aren't going anywhere until you talk with the physician," he said.

The room to the hospital was so very white that I felt as if it enveloped me. It was midday. It had to be St. Matthew Hospital. *I am on a high floor of this hospital*, I thought as I looked out the long, rectangular side window viewing the adjacent light gray wall with windows. At the end of that wall to the left of my hospital room window was the entirely lightish gray sky.

As I turned, I noticed Jonathan was seated on the square, light green chair with wooden arms and legs. He buried his hands in his face, which gave me a view of his coarse, curly hair. I loved the texture of Jonathan's hair. He would brush it sometimes, actually making sound. That was what drew me to really notice Jonathan's hair, the sound he made with a brush.

As the physician entered from the door across the room, Jonathan arose, walked toward me, and settled, standing, in front of the clouded window.

"You have an appointment for your return visit next Tuesday," the physician stated and also explained that he had written a prescription.

From my view above the metal bars to my right, I could see the square-tiled ceiling and the doctor's head atop a light blue dress shirt and white jacket as he briskly left the hospital room.

Jonathan turned, reached for the cord, and closed the drapes, producing a newly formed absence of light.

"You are going to be all right, Sheila," Jonathan stated as he walked from the window over to my bed. "How do you feel now?"

"I feel somewhat better, Jonathan."

"The nurse stated that you will be released in the morning. I spoke with her on the way into your room this morning. You are going to have to go to the clinic for a therapy visit with the psychiatrist, who was just here earlier."

"I will?"

"Yes, what he was speaking of was a follow-up visit. The doctor wants to get to the root of what is the main problem, why everything went wrong all of a sudden. I have known you for quite a while, Sheila, and nothing like this has ever happened. I did not have any indication that you were this depressed. If I did, I would have gotten you help earlier and would not have let you stay alone last night."

"Oh, Jonathan, I just had a few drinks," I stated. "Understand? One drink led to another, and before I knew it, I was out of it."

"You were really out of it when I arrived, but do not ponder what happened," he said. "We are going to take it one step at a time—one day at a time—and you're going to be just fine."

"It shouldn't really take a long amount of time to get back to normal. As a matter of fact, I feel like I'm back to normal as we speak. Why do I have to take medication? I really don't think much is wrong with me. I mean, I have adjusted to the voices over the years, and since I have been here in the hospital I have not heard anything out of the ordinary."

"Yes, but it has not been long since I found you after such a horrible event," Jonathan said. "Sheila, from now on, you can call me if you ever need to talk about anything at all or if you feel depressed. However, the only way to alleviate hearing things out of the ordinary is to take the medication your doctor prescribed for you. Promise?"

"OK, Jonathan. I promise."

"And don't drink alcohol, like I tried to get you to understand last night," he said. "By all means, you can't drink with your medication."

"I promise."

"Good, because I care about you, girl," he continued. "I know that you're all alone here in Sommerville—without friends and family. Yet, that's not the reason that we have become best friends. What can I say, Sheila? You're attractive, intelligent, and successful. You're always there when I need solutions to answers to my questions regarding those deadbeats at the firm. You don't know how every time I ask your advice on my issues with those deadbeats, your answer is always accurate. I've told you, Sheila, how you have gotten me through so many situations that I had to get through just to maintain my reputation."

"You have told me that you appreciate my advice, Jonathan," I said.

"Not to mention how you keep me feeling like being a black man is an honor. A lot of brothers don't know it's an honor to be a black man, and you showed me different. I couldn't have escaped feeling somewhat inferior, seeing the state of my race in America—continued struggle but really no progression for the masses. Most black women I am in contact with think that I am some square know-it-all if they are a black woman, but you never did. They think I am some uncaring sell-out. But they do not really know me. I am rich, but I tithe every Sunday and also give back to the poor. Under their breath they call me a smart you-know-what if they are a racist, jealous of my success and intelligence. God made me a black man."

"Well, you are about to preach, my brother," I exclaimed.

"God set me rich."

"Well," I stated, ringing out my word like I was in church service.

"No, I am not going to preach, girl. What I am going to do is let your ears rest from my jibber-jabber. I will be back to pick you up when you are released in the morning."

When Jonathan left I realized my conversations with him had uplifted him and actually helped him in his career. I also realized that confiding in each other grew a close bond of friendship.

Jonathan arrived in this world in a poor upbringing. However, like he stated, he turned out a rich man. He was empathetic to the needs of poor black men due to his roots.

As for me, I felt as though there was no hope in changing the auditory interruptions that were frightening and cut into my daily life without advance notice. As I pondered my present state I considered the voices from past to present and determined that they had worsened.

I was thoroughly examined physically and mentally during the process of my transition of becoming well. I was medicated and didn't hear a manipulating voice throughout my stay at St. Matthew Hospital. I was encouraged to seek therapy, and I felt that it would brighten my life, which was improving steadily.

Valencia

AFTER MY HOSPITAL stay I arrived home in healthy spirits. Yet, when Jonathan departed, I recognized the emptiness of an otherwise unoccupied home and my present isolation in my dwelling place.

How I had gotten so far in life as a successful investment banker and not acquired an immediate family? No children. Listen to me, "acquired." Well, how else would I have obtained a husband and children without acquiring or obtaining? I was entirely too busy to fit those two aspects in my life, but I probably should have, else I would not have been considering them in that moment. I should have a husband, a handsome, loving husband and children to nurture. Feed. Bathe. Pamper. Clothe. Teach.

The phone rang.

"Hello."

"Hi, Sheila."

"Jonathan."

"I'm checking in with you on my way back home," he said. "You all right?"

"Yes, just transitioning back."

"Sure you're all right?" he asked. "Because I could head back there and stay a few days to keep you company."

"Why don't you," I said. "I have never been so lonely in my entire life."

"OK, Sheila," he said. "Let me grab some things, and I'll see you this evening."

"What would I do without you, Jon?"

"I feel exactly the same about you, Sheila."

I hung up. *Something about that man makes everything in my life perfect. His parents raised him absolutely perfectly.*

I twisted the top to the plastic brown-colored bottle and gently tapped out a round, inscribed pill. I placed the pill on the countertop as I filled ice and water into my glass. I swallowed the pill, continuing to drink until I had finished the entire glass of water.

I had officially started my prescription. *Why am I taking psychiatric medication?*

I entered my living room, and in peering out of the dark wooden framed picture window, I easily viewed the all-too-familiar green-yellowish colored bushes lining the far outer edge of the back entrance into the back of my condominium. *I'll take a short nap before Jonathan arrives*, I thought as I placed my sunglasses on and walked into the sunroom. I sat down on the white wicker chair and in no time dozed off.

I awoke abruptly to the sound of Jonathan shouting my name at the back of the gazebo. When I opened my eyes I saw light from a flashlight dancing unsteadily. I had slept for hours, and Jonathan was outside the gazebo insistently calling my name.

"I'm awake, Jonathan," I stated, arising from the chair.

"You're asleep out here, Sheila?"

"Yes, Jonathan." I unlatched the screened door into the gazebo. "I fell asleep for hours. Come in, Jonathan. Glad to have you for a while."

Jonathan walked into my living room holding a small suitcase, and he continued into the adjacent guest bedroom.

"I take it you will want me to make myself at home here?" he stated.

"Yes, Jonathan," I answered.

"Listen, Sheila, you might need some more rest," he said. "Sorry if I disturbed you on the way in. I was at the front of your condo, and when you didn't answer I made it to the back. See how ingenious I am?"

"Yep," I said as I had made my way to the stairs. When I had reached the top of the stairs, Jonathan was at the landing.

"Sweet dreams, girl."

"Off to la-la land," I stated.

I awoke the next morning to the aroma of maple bacon. The sun shone brightly as I opened my eyes and turned to view the clear blue sky centered between my white ruffled curtains pulled to each side.

Jonathan entered my room with a small wooden breakfast table under one arm, which he arranged on each side of my lap. From a platter in his other hand he placed on it silverware, a glass of orange juice, a cup of coffee, and a plate filled with French toast with melting butter and syrup, maple bacon, fried eggs, and a fruit medley consisting of strawberries, raspberries, and blueberries. Jonathan sat down on the foot of my bed.

"How beautiful of you, Jonathan," I said.

"I get up at the crack of dawn, girl," he said. "Plus, I had to make you breakfast."

"I don't know if I can eat all of it," I stated as I cut a small piece of French toast. "This is delicious! It melts in my mouth, Jonathan."

"Did you eat yet?" I asked.

"Yes," he said.

The phone rang.

"Hello," Jonathan said. "Leclaire residence."

"This is Valencia Russell. Sheila there? I didn't know she had a man around."

"Yes, she is. I'm her friend Jonathan," he stated and handed me the phone.

"Hello," I said.

Jonathan sat back down and rubbed my legs as he crooned, "Massage," in a soothing tone.

"Negro, you better git out of my room!" I yelled.

"Valencia," I yelled into the phone. "How you doin', girl? I was waiting for your phone call. I didn't have your number. I called Allie the other day, and she stated that she didn't have your number. Girl, it has been years since I have been in touch with you, hasn't it?"

I hadn't heard Valencia's voice in all these years. "Allie is Allie girl," Valencia stated.

"Yes, she is still the same!" I added. "She is entirely too busy in everybody's business, but when she is called on the carpet for starting so much mess, she acts like she doesn't know what is going on."

We stated at the same time, "But everybody knows," both giggling.

"Yeah, we all know how she is, and she even goes so far as to stop us from talking. I would have called you before now if it weren't for Allie," I continued. "Wait until I see her. She is supposed to be visiting DC next spring."

"How are you?" she questioned.

"Managing well, Val," I said. "I'm still alone."

"So am I," Valencia stated.

"Haven't found him yet, girl, and I probably never will," I said.

"Sheila, do they have all the good men or what?" Valencia added. "Every man that interests me is in a relationship."

"I don't know. I haven't looked for nobody, Val, seeing that I have acquired a very good friend, Jonathan. He is one of the best picks in Sommerville. You know me. I wouldn't have it any other way, girl. He is super fine, Val."

"Sounds like you got luck, Sheila," she said.

"Valencia," I stated softly. "If you do not quit being nosy about my Negro…"

"Val, I have to ask you something," I said.

"Let me have it," Valencia said.

"Last night I had a peculiar dream. I was up at St. Matthew's for a few days to get my mind right."

"I know, Sheila," Valencia said.

"I've been going to a therapist since first leaving Sommerville," she continued. "Girl, since I moved out on the west coast I could not adjust to a different life here. I love the east coast. Do you understand, Sheila?"

"You didn't like Sommerville?" I questioned.

"No, Sheila," she said. "We socialized a lot and spent a lot of time working with youth in the community organization. That was our only way of coping. You were younger than me, Sheila. So many things went on that you knew nothing about. That's why we participated in the community group—to get our minds off something else other than the painful memories, anticipating that we could adjust to a peaceful youth. We tried to cover painful memories by helping those poor youngsters— and we were youngsters ourselves."

"Val, was I ever hospitalized?" I asked. "Because I dreamed—"

"Yea, after you got your royal butt kicked, girl," Valencia stated. "They kicked the mess out of you. They beat you up so bad."

"When was that? How old was I? I don't remember ever being beat up. By whom?" I asked.

"You were about four. We were down playing by the river on the other side of the park. It was some distance from the park, and I hate to say it, Sheila, but we drifted down there from the sidewalk that the ladies would always walk with their strollers, except we kept on past the trees and into the field—Allie, Mary, you, and me. It was really hilly in Sommerville."

"Still is," I stated.

"We ventured on down by the river," Valencia continued. "Sheila, I guess we always viewed those woods from where we played, and we must have been inquisitive as to what was there. There were trees all around, except it was cleaned out over by the river."

"What happened?" I asked.

"Some boys, about six or seven boys, came over by the river to fish. Soon as they set eyes on us, they went to screaming. They yelled, 'Get out of here! Get away from here!' We went to racing out of that place all except you. Didn't know you were missing until we were back at the park. We took off running to your house—up the stairs to your parents' house. Your parents opened the door, and we were just screaming. We figured you had slowed down running. We stayed at your parents' house when they went to look for you."

"That must have been what I dreamed," I stated.

"They beat you, Sheila," Valencia said sobbing. "Sheila, that is why I left Sommerville. You don't remember, Sheila. I know you don't remember."

"No, I don't remember, Val," I said.

Whole

WHEN I HUNG up the phone with Valencia, my first thought was how I was unaware of this occurrence in my early childhood. I pondered, reaching as far back as possible as my memory could allow, past my first day of work life, past my high school and college years, past the community organization, and even past memories of my siblings, past vacations, and birthday parties. I considered every memory of childhood during the timeframe that Valencia had stated I had been beaten. Interestingly, I could not envision or remember any clue from my past that would validate her recollection. Not that I wouldn't believe Valencia. If there were anyone who would tell me the truth, it would be Valencia, although there were others who wouldn't lie to me, including friends and family.

I don't remember my father or my twin brothers ever fishing in the woods. They never went near the woods. There was a tree house that my father built in one of the oak trees that they used to play in when the twins were about ten years old. Yet, before that they used to play in the backyard. My mother was always outside with us. In addition, there was a host of my friends that used to come to my house to play in the backyard.

I had always thought when I got older that my mother was tied down watching my twin brothers due to the difficulty of raising two toddlers concurrently. In spite of it, she never one day appeared not to enjoy motherhood. She provided very patient mothering. When we were done playing in the evenings right before dinner was served, she would bathe us and put us in our sleep clothes prior to eating dinner. After a long day of play, we almost literally fell asleep at the dinner table. However, that would have never happened due to her relishing cuisine. Today I wonder how she finished supper when she spent the majority of time with us during the day. Each one of her meals was exceptional, in comparison to an experienced chef-for-hire. Interestingly, she never repeated meals for at least two months, and to this day I enjoy all foods. She properly introduced every kind of meat, poultry, vegetable, fruit, dessert, etc. I surmise that she arose early to cook and clean because our home was immaculate.

"Sheila?" Jonathan asked as he entered my room. "You have your doctor's visit at 2:00 p.m."

"Yes, Jonathan, my first therapy visit," I said. "I am going to shower, and I'll be ready in a flash."

"All right, I'm going to be downstairs in the sitting room," he stated. "I'll drive you into town."

Since I had lost track of time, I quickly gathered my apparel. I was feeling somewhat nervous about the newness and felt like telling Jonathan that I didn't want to do this therapy visit. It's horrible to feel nervous and have to rush.

"Hey, Jonathan!" I called.

"Yes, Sheila."

"I feel like I'm on my way to an interview," I said, and before I could finish my sentence, Jonathan was standing in my doorway.

"Just stay calm, girl," he said. "I know that this is a big step and difficult, but it's for the better. You can only improve. Plus, I have to admit you look like you're doing much better compared to when you were up at the hospital yesterday. I'm sure that the doctor will find so as well."

"Guess what?" I asked, smiling.

"What, Sheila?"

"I'm not nervous anymore."

Jonathan moved closer. "You aren't?" he said, and smacked a kiss on my lips.

"Ahhh," I yelled. "You kissed me, Jonathan!"

I raced to the front door laughing and pulled it open. I stood in the front door and yelled, "Jonathan stole a kiss! Na-na-na na-na! Jonathan kissed me!" I continued.

Jonathan ran past me to the car, opening my car door and stating, "About time you kissed me, girl."

"Jonathan Stevenson," I stated, "You're going to smack a kiss on my pretty pink lips and then drive me into town? Good timing?"

Jonathan stood in his tracks with a beautiful smile forming the lower half of his bronze complexion. "Come on, sweetie," he said. "Get in the car, babe."

"With those pretty legs," he said as I walked down the stairs to my porch.

"Jonathan!" I said. "You kissed me. Then you complimented me. The rate this is going we're going to end up at city hall!"

"Perfecto," Jonathan said as we drove off into town.

When we arrived at the office of Dr. Theodore Lewis we waited approximately ten minutes before the door opened to the back office and the registration clerk called my name. I walked alongside the registration clerk as she led me to my psychiatrist's office. I entered the office of Dr. Lewis, who was waiting in the doorway.

"Please have a seat, Sheila," he said.

"How have you been feeling since you were in the hospital?"

"Better," I stated vibrantly.

"Today I am going to find out more about what exactly is going on with you and your background," he said. "This might be a long visit because I have very in-depth questions for you to answer," he continued. "However, depending on your strength, we can finish on another day if you choose."

Dr. Lewis went over some general questioning. He asked about my early childhood, family, use of drugs and alcohol, occupation, suicidal thoughts, voices and hearing things, and relationships with friends and family. I went over each question normally and rather quickly.

I told Dr. Lewis that I had never attempted to kill myself or at least not thought I had. I told him that I thought I took medication the night before I was hospitalized because I had a headache from what I recalled.

During my visit Dr. Lewis was particularly interested in knowing about the voices that I heard. He stated that I was hallucinating. I told him that I had suffered hearing voices ever since I was little and recalled my first memory of a hallucination.

I told Dr. Lewis what had happened when I was six and a half years old. "I remember it was six months before my birthday in May because my father used to always ask in advance what I wanted for my birthday," I stated.

"He always wanted my birthday to be special, so he did not intermingle play toys, books, trips, etc. that provided fun and excitement in the summer months with the special gift that I requested for my birthday in January," I continued. "At the end of the summer

I would always have something to look forward to at the beginning of the new year in which my birthday also fell.

"When I was six and a half years old, there were tall oak trees in back of our home in Sommerville. I used to run through the trees, ending up in a wide expanse of field."

As I retold the event to Dr. Lewis, it was just as if I was back in time when I was six and a half.

"I told my daddy in June of 1978 I wanted a sled for my birthday so I could slide down this hilly hill. As I ran through the field beyond the woods I started to skip merrily as I thought about the fun I would have with that sled. When I got to the middle of the field, I always turned back to see the tall oak trees, which looked dense after I had gotten to the middle of the field rather than when I started out running through them. I remember thinking, "Mama is going to have twins. That means two."

"We had just gotten back from town, and riding in that back seat of my daddy's car was not as open as now. I took off running to the end of the field where I got to the road at the top of another hilly area. I could see the swings going high and a couple of children lined up to climb the stairs to the slide. A girl was going down the slide. There were two ladies walking with carriages on the next street in back of the park. I ran down the hill and stopped again just as I reached the park. *I'll go on the slide*, I thought. I ran to the slide and was next in line. I started to climb the stairs in back of the boy in front of me, being careful not to get too close to his shoes as he steadily climbed upward. It was a tall slide. He sat down on the slide and put his hands on his thighs and slid down. He yelled, 'Whoosh!' After he had reached the bottom of the slide and was walking back around, I sat down and slid down. When I reached the bottom I saw my friend Mary. I yelled out to her.

"'Hi, Sheila.'

"'I'm going again.'

"I climbed the ladder again and slid down. When I got to the bottom I yelled, 'Mary!'

"She stated, 'Do the swing!'

"I ran over to Mary and ran past her swing when her swing was going backward into the air.

"I took the dark grayish chains in each hand and sat down on the dark-green swing seat after I had gone backward a few steps and pushed my short legs forward to swing forward. I swung higher and higher. It was about the fifth time up that I got really scared on the swing.

"I heard something say, 'Stop!'

"I slowed down on the swing, looking through the park to see if I could hear the person who shouted at me. I did not see anyone but children and a few women.

"I heard again, 'Stop!'

"When the swing stopped I took off running to the top of the hill by the street.

"The voice was repeating. 'Stop! Stop! Stop! Stop!'

"'Leave me 'lone,' I yelled.

"I kept yelling, yelling, and yelling. A lady had raced beside me trying to calm me down. Someone had run to get my daddy, who picked me up and carried me across the street through the field and oak trees home."

I felt very tired and drained after telling Dr. Lewis my first account of a hallucinatory event from my early childhood. My psychiatrist was the first person that I told. I don't know the reason that I didn't tell Valencia yesterday. I guess the reason that I didn't was because we were chatting of the tragedy that happened a little

over two years before my first hallucination. I must
have had a memory lapse and forgotten the beating
that she described early on in my childhood because
in thinking back about the hallucination I didn't
recall knowing about what happened even during that
time. I had told my psychiatrist that a longtime friend,
Valencia, had informed me what had happened when
I was four years old and that I was beaten until I was
unconscious. *I'll have to give my mother a phone call
soon to figure out if she can fill in the blanks of such a
tragic time of my past*, I thought.

At the conclusion of my first therapy visit Dr. Lewis
told me to continue medication and that it was good
the voices had subsided. He said to call his office if
they reoccurred. He stated that he felt that I was doing
better. He also stated that it was favorable to have a
close friend such as Jonathan, who could help me
through such a difficult time in my life.

"You are going to get everything together, Sheila.
You are a very intelligent woman, and from what you
have told me today you are piecing together facts
from your childhood and answering questions from
your past. That is something that I could never do
for you, and as a result you are developing a form
of therapeutic history for yourself. When you finish
contacting your friends and family and actually
discovering what your past truthfully holds, you will
be able to move forward in adjusting properly. I am
sure. Talk with whomever you need to talk with, and if
you happen to run into certain difficulties with respect
to historical information, give me a call," Dr. Lewis
said and handed me his card. "I have been in the area
as a clinical psychologist and resident of Sommerville
since the late 1960s, and I might be able to help you

out if need be. However, I am sure you will be able to handle your discovery."

Jonathan and I left the doctor's office, and I explained to him on the way home that I was feeling even better, that I was fitting everything that happened to me together like missing pieces of a puzzle. I explained to Jonathan that I had always remembered hearing that voice when I was playing at the park that day, but I never really considered it a hallucination.

"Get you some rest when you get home, Sheila," Jonathan said. "I understand it must be very difficult for you to remember your painful past, especially because of it being so vivid, almost as if you are reliving it, as you described. I feel so sorry for you. I don't know what I would have done if that happened to my daughter. I am sure that your parents were torn up about your mental state in the years following what those low-lives did to you."

"I am going to call Mama soon, Jon."

"I have a feeling that she has more to the story than even Valencia retold this morning," I stated as Jonathan turned into the front driveway of my condominium. We both got out of the car and made our way into the house. Jonathan turned on the television in the living room and was tuned into the six o'clock news stories as I climbed the stairs to the second floor.

Clover

A s I reached my bedroom door I heard a voice. *Sweet dreams.* It was a woman's voice that I definitely recognized.

"I am through," I stated louder than I wanted.

"What did you say, Sheila?" Jonathan stated.

Jonathan was nearer than I thought and therefore more than likely he had heard me.

"Just talking aloud, Jonathan."

"Oh really?"

"Yes. I do it all the time. I forgot you were here. I didn't scare you, did I?"

"No, Sheila, you didn't scare me."

"Jonathan, did I ever show you pictures of my old friends from Sistering Mission?" I asked.

"You never did," he said. "I would like to take a look."

I walked into my bedroom, continuing to the foot of my mahogany bed, opened the top wooden door of my chest, and took out the photo album atop several boxes of memorabilia.

"Have a seat, Jonathan," I stated as I sat down on the blue couch adjacent the window in my bedroom. I handed Jonathan the album while he was being seated.

Jonathan carefully opened the light yellow cover to my photo album with pages that were lightly fading to an off-white color. He continued flipping pages until he had reached some articles regarding chorus and speech competitions that my high school teams had won.

"You were on the speech team and in chorus?"

"Yes."

Jonathan continued flipping pages and stopped abruptly at one of them.

"You are as beautiful as you were in high school! You have not changed much, just ripened. You were a foxy girl!"

He studied the photo on the page. "These were your friends?"

"Yes. That's Mary, Valencia, Allie, and me. We were at the annual picnic in Washington, DC, for the community organization.

"That's Valencia that phoned today?" Jonathan asked.

"Yes."

"She really looked afro-centric for the 1980s."

"Valencia was very strong minded, or should I say positioned. She was also involved in sports. If she believed in someone or something she fought to the bitter end for that person or cause. She is a high school mathematics teacher in Los Angeles."

"That's Mary," I stated while pointing to the picture. "She is married in Atlanta, a happy homemaker. None of us has children. Mary has tried continually for several years to have a baby. She has tried fertility drugs. Yet, she is infertile."

"That is too bad," Jonathan said. "Must be a terrible situation to get hitched and then not be able to conceive. She looks of mixed heritage."

"Yes, her father was Caucasian."

"Oh, she is really mixed," Jonathan stated.

"You would have thought her features would have been more slimmed down with a Caucasian father,"

Jonathan continued while raking his right hand through his short, curly afro.

"I guess you never know with genes which ones are going to take effect," I stated.

"Her father, Mr. Jacobs, was so nice, Jonathan," I continued. "He was really close to Valencia's parents. He taught English at our high school."

"And there is Allie," I said. "Allie was very well liked. She was our senior class president. Allie and I are the same age. She modeled and also was a cheerleader. She owns a marketing firm. She is married and lives in Dallas."

"She was stunning!" Jonathan exclaimed. "You all were knockouts indeed!"

"That was us back then," I said. "We spent most of our time outside of high school participating in Sistering Mission's activities. We raised funds to meet causes for our intercity peers in Washington, DC. We also were involved in activities related to mentoring, socialization, and education."

"Jonathan?" I said.

"You are getting very sleepy?" He stated.

I chuckled, "I'm getting very *sleepy*." I drew out the last word to emphasize my tiredness. "Time for a nap, Jonathan."

"Get some rest, Sheila," Jonathan stated. "I'm going to prepare some vittles while you take a nap, hon."

As Jonathan was leaving my bedroom I had placed the photo album into my wooden chest. He closed the room door, and I lay down onto my bed facing the window. The curtains were still pulled open, revealing the sunset sky, which darkened to a starry night as I drifted off to sleep.

Miss Charlotte

A FEW HOURS LATER, I awakened pondering over one voice in my dream.

"That was the voice I heard after I left the doctor's office when I returned home," I stated. "She looked just like Allie's mother in the dream."

Since I had a bad habit of forgetting if I did not refresh my memory soon after awakening, I quickly recaptured my dream.

My dream had taken me to a bar with a very dim lighting. It seemed as though there were no lights but for a few candles placed on the shelves on the wall behind the bar in between empty alcohol bottles refilled with water and other small ceramics.

There was a cocktail waitress with a large, curly afro. Interestingly, her hair was such a good grade, but she had managed to shape it into a beautifully formed afro with soft, curly locks.

She was a lighter complexioned Negro woman the shade of a mulatto. She was a shapely woman with an hourglass figure. She was smiling with a perfect set of teeth, as if she had remarkably completed a dental treatment.

She was wearing a black, short, shimmery dress. A man was seated at the end of the bar with his back turned toward me. In my dream I walked slowly into the bar and noticed a man smiling at me as I passed his seat. There was also a man seated further down from me talking to a lady in a red dress with her hair in bouncy, jet-black curls. They were laughing and talking.

She motioned to the man she was talking to and turned and walked toward me. She stopped beside me and stated, "You from around here?"

"Sommerville, Virginia," I stated, continuing past the gentleman who accompanied her, and sat down at the far end of the bar. In doing so I gained a side view of the first man that I had passed on the way. He continued to smile and gaze at the mulatto lady. The mulatto lady kept chatting with him, telling her story. When she was completed she looked at him, smiling.

"Go on and sing my song," he told her.

She sung "Dream My Days Away" beautifully, like an accomplished singer.

"Been alone so long. Never here to stay. I dream my days away." The sound drifted through my mind and filled me with peace.

What beautiful music in my dream, I thought as I heard a light rapping on my room door.

"Sheila, dear."

"Yes, Jonathan. Come in."

"I'm going to run out to the store," Jonathan said. "Be right back. Care for anything? You were out of a few items."

"No thanks, Jon," I said. "I'm going to give Valencia a call. I have some more questions for her."

"All right, Sheila," Jonathan said.

I rose up into a seated position on the bed with my back against my mahogany headboard. I opened the top drawer of my nightstand beside my bed and located my address book.

"Let's see. Valencia Russell."

I dialed her number, and it switched over to voice mail. I was just getting ready to hang up the phone when her phone message stopped and I heard Valencia's voice.

"Hello," Valencia said.

"Yes, Val," I said. "This is Sheila."

"Hey, girl," she said. "How are you?"

"Good," I said. "I'm much better. I had a successful visit with my psychiatrist, and he stated that I will be just all right, girl."

"Yeah?" she stated. "Sounds very good, Sheila. What else have you been up to?"

"Well, just resting and sorting through my past, trying to put everything into place," I said. "I think I will be happier if I can get some closure by just knowing all there is to know regarding my past, because it does not feel good to have unanswered questions, especially from my formative years.

"I just feel sorry for that girl that got beat," I continued. "I refer to the timeframe when I was up to six years old as someone else because I do not remember my entire childhood during that time. I feel sorry for her, and my goal is to remember what happened, because aside from that pain there had to be good memories. Yet, I do not have a clue as to much regarding my life then."

"Well girl, I wish you luck on that," Valencia said. "It's gonna be difficult. I can't shed any light on that other than what I have told you so far. I have told you all I can remember. It would be different if we had some type of association during that time so that we could have been more vocal after that horrible event took place, but all I know is that we stayed in the house. All of your whereabouts were monitored extremely closely, even throughout high school.

"Each of us—Allie, Mary, and me—*knew* what happened to you, Sheila, and it was always in the back of our minds," Valencia continued. "There was never closure because we could never understand why they did not catch those cruel boys that beat you up!

"We always knew—at least, I always knew—what happened because my parents would always get to talking about what happened to 'Valencia's friend Sheila,' and my dad was very close to your father," she said.

"Your dad worked very closely with that detective in following up with your case downtown," she said. "However, it was unresolved.

"Sheila, I can't say that our parents didn't prevent anything else from occurring," she said. "Did you know that their network was very intricate?

"They had every parent's phone number on a roster," she continued. "Even Mary's parents' maid was to call to her parents if she wasn't at home promptly.

"I guess they set up things that way because there was no closure to a host of tragedies that we encountered during our childhood."

"Valencia?" I asked.

"Yes, girl," she said.

"Before I called you I ended up remembering a dream I had of a lady in a bar in DC," I said.

"What did she look like?" she asked.

"Actually, she really resembled Allie's mother," I said.

"Allie's mother?" Valencia questioned.

"Yes, you know our friend Allie!" I said. "What are you talking about Allie's mother? You know Allie's mother, Valencia."

"Before you begin, Sheila, and get totally ticked off with me, I have to tell you about who you are referring to as Allie's mother," she said.

"What?" I asked.

"The lady that we know as Allie's mother is really her grandmother," Valencia stated.

"And?"

"Her mother was murdered."

"What?" I asked. "Am I hearing you right? Allie's mother was murdered? And Miss Charlotte was Allie's grandmother?"

"Yes, Sheila, another tragic event in our circle of friends' lives," she said.

"Does Allie know?" I asked.

"Yes, she found out a few years ago," Valencia said. "Miss Charlotte decided to tell her because she had taken ill."

"She never really knew her mother. She stayed with Miss Charlotte for all those years thinking that she was her mother," I said.

"Yes," Valencia said. "Allie's mother was murdered in Washington, DC. Allie's grandmother took Allie in when she moved to Sommerville after her mother was murdered. They never caught who did it."

"I guess that *was* the right way to handle the situation seeing that she was quite young," I said. "Strangely enough, she should have remembered her mother. Don't you have memories of your mother at an early age, Val?" I asked.

"Indeed yes, Sheila," she said.

"Maybe she was attached to her grandmother when she came to live in Sommerville," I said.

"Allie's grandmother just raised her as her own," Valencia stated. "She did not want to think about her daughter being deceased and raised Allie like she was her daughter, Angela."

"Allie told me that her grandmother spent most of her time in her home worrying and crying about her daughter, Angela," she continued. "Allie said that sometimes she would call her Angela. When I found out that her mother was murdered I was shocked and full of questions just like you, Sheila, because we grew up knowing Miss Charlotte and thought that was her mother. Miss Charlotte raised her like her own daughter."

The front door bell sounded as I hung up the phone with Valencia. I walked into the hallway, continuing down the stairs to the front door. Turning the knob felt like turning the years of my life. I was living in the present but still turning over unanswered questions from my past, all while dealing with the reality facing me that some individuals' lives are not perfect. Take Allie's life, for example. I had to live with my early life's events, no matter how difficult, just as Allie did. *Gosh, what do I say to Allie now that I know this new terrible news?* I wondered.

Angela

"HELLO, JONATHAN," I stated when I opened the door. "My, did you buy the whole store?"

"Tried to," Jonathan said, carrying several bags. "You look dazed, girl. Something wrong?"

"Yeah, I just received some terrible news," I stated. "I spoke with Valencia while you were gone. She broke some real sad news to me. She told me after all these years that Miss Charlotte is not Allie's mother."

"You are referring to the mixed girl?" Jonathan questioned. "When we went through the pictures?"

"Yeah, my friend Allie," I said. "Miss Charlotte is her grandmother. Her mother's name is Angela.

"Worse yet," I continued, "Allie's real mother was murdered!"

"Murdered?" Jonathan asked. "How long ago?"

"It had to be in the 1970s, because that's when Allie moved to Sommerville to stay with Miss Charlotte," I stated.

"Astounding!" Jonathan exclaimed. "She kept that secret from her all those years."

"That was exactly my thought when I found out," I said. "Yet, Valencia stated that Miss Charlotte was so distraught and seemingly doubtful or unbelieving."

"Miss Charlotte did not want to accept her daughter's death?" Jonathan asked.

"Yes, she treated Allie like her daughter," I said.

"That was her granddaughter," he said.

"She even used to slip and call her Angela," I said.

"That's so sad, Sheila," he said.

"Isn't it, Jonathan?" I stated. "What do I say to Allie when we talk?"

"Tell her how you feel, Sheila," Jonathan said. "Tell her that you are very sad to hear about what happened to her real birth mother. When did she find out?"

"Valencia said only a couple of years ago," I said.

"If she was not strong her whole life will be affected by that news," Jonathan said.

"She must be thankful to God for having Miss Charlotte to raise her after her mother's death," he continued. "God provided protection to her life from unforeseeable harm after her mother's death."

"Jonathan, you are such a faithful man," I said.

"Sheila, I learned to have a prayer life," he said. "My mama put me down on my knees every night to say my prayers. Hey, I made it through law school, but law school was a cinch compared to the realization that God desired me to keep praying," he said. "I keep praying. God keeps answering my prayers. I keep praying, and God opens up doors."

"Amen," I stated.

Allie

"Hello," I said.

"Hello, may I ask who is calling?"

"Allie, this is Sheila," I said.

"Hello, Sheila," Allie answered. "It has been quite some time. It has been several months since you phoned. I believe it was last fall that you phoned me. Do you know that I almost didn't receive your call today? I was busy—extremely busy with several activities that you would probably consider mundane. Sheila, I had a meeting this morning with my committee at church. After that, I traveled downtown for several hours to work on budgetary concerns. I met with the golf club at Oak Meadows Country Club. At noon, we decided to have lunch at Ginger's Ridge. After that, the club decided to do some shopping in downtown Dallas. And I made it back home to rest a few hours before I got dressed for a dinner party. Reginald is on his way back from downtown from picking up his tuxedo. So, Sheila, I have been busy today.

"However, I am rather pleased to hear your voice, my dear friend. I haven't found friends like you all, and I don't slip in and out of several walks of life. I maintain the same class, similar to out east. It was very easy for me to fit into Dallas's elite. You know I would not have it any other way. Nevertheless, these socially elite women are absent when it comes to class. That is why I have to go to church, Sheila. These women in the golf club sneak around with each other's partners and continue to lift their noses high to the air, thinking that no one knows and no one will discover their improprieties.

"Yet, you know me, Sheila. I am a social butterfly. I uncover untruths, so they do not reach my Reginald. Sheila, what would I do if one of my golf buddies snuck into my relationship with Reginald? Reginald has had numerous instances of falling through the inevitable mistresses' nets. How is it I continually have preventive measures? He is not trustworthy. Sheila, can you imagine a pre-cheater? That's Reginald. That's what I have, Sheila. Don't fret about being tied down as of yet, or ever, Sheila. There is nothing worse than continually existing just because Reginald didn't get caught yet. The high point of my marriage with Reginald is the mental tickle I receive from knowledge of his misadventures. You would think that he would have pals that would hip him to the process, but he does not. I guess I should have been a detective, Sheila.

"Oh, I am sorry girl. It's just that I can really only take so much of Reginald before I feel like tossing him out like an old pair of shoes. You know, when you go through the closet and can't find your shoes and get to tossing through that mess?

"Sheila, I just keep talking, girl. What is your life like now? When I spoke with you last fall I didn't get to cover what I wanted to due to the busy nature of my life, as I have explained, my dear friend."

"Allie, I hope everything is truly all right with you, from the bottom of my heart," I said. "I got a lot of love in the bottom of my heart for you," I continued. "When I talked with Val today she filled me in on what happened to your real mother, and I'm so sorry."

"I didn't know who my mother was," Allie snapped. "I was too young.

"Oh, I'm sorry, Sheila," Allie stated. "What did Val tell you exactly?

"Never mind," Allie said. "She must have told you everything I told her. Did Val tell you I was upset?

"My mother was a nasty tramp," Allie snapped again.

"I am sorry, Sheila," Allie stated as her voice changed, while moaning. "She was not anything if she was a heroin addict.

"Miss Charlotte told me my real mother was an owner of a nightclub in Philadelphia," Allie continued. "She ended up meeting and dating a musical composer who ended up being my father.

"Miss Charlotte said his name was Emmanuel Patterson," Allie continued. "She got hooked on heroin when their marriage eventually failed, and she moved to Washington, DC, to live with Miss Charlotte, my grandmother.

"Miss Charlotte moved to Sommerville after my mother was murdered," she said.

"How is Miss Charlotte?" I asked.

"She's doing well. You know she is well off. She gets around OK. There is nothing wrong with her, excluding a little touch of arthritis. She travels abroad for the most part, and she makes it through the States as well. I keep in contact with Miss Charlotte. What would I have done without her?

"Sheila, my mother was totally different than Miss Charlotte raised her. One thing I am lucky for is that she gave me some information on my dad's whereabouts. She always kept up with him. He remarried and settled up in New Jersey. When I first called him I spoke with one of his daughters, and it seemed like I was talking to myself. I didn't know who she was until Dad told me that I had seven brothers and sisters. He is well off. He struck it rich with his music business. He supported me all my life, and I didn't know he was sending significant amounts of money to Miss Charlotte. She saved a lot of it and handed it over to me when I finished college. That is why I shouldn't be chasing Reginald around. I have more money than him, and with the prenuptial he will not get anything when he philanders with his new sashayin' floozy.

"Anyway, dad is going to come and stay with us for about a month next Christmas," Allie said. "I do not know how I'm going to keep up with what Reginald is doing. Guess I'm going to have to hire a private investigator during that time, because he would luck up then with all that time on his hands."

"Allie, you got him under control, girl," I said.

"Yeah, Sheila," she stated, chuckling, and then stopped laughing. "Maybe I better hire the private eye in September, because he will have the house to himself when I travel to San Jose."

"Maybe you should," I said.

Mama

O N SEPTEMBER 9, a few months later, I reached for my telephone off of my nightstand as I snapped shut the last suitcase I had finished packing. I wondered who was calling me right before I was about to exit my home on the way to the airport.

"Hello?" I asked.

"Hello, Sheila," Mama stated.

"Hi, Mama," I stated. "I have not spoken with you in months, Mama. I was going to call you, and then several months passed. I have been healing."

"Healing?" Mama questioned. "Mind playing tricks on you? You all right now I bet."

"Yes, I am all right now," I said. "Jonathan helped me through the ordeal. I feel like I had a nervous breakdown."

"You found out everything, Sheila?" Mama asked. "Need me to fill in the blanks or do some more explaining?" Mama continued. "I bet you found out enough from your past to set your life straight so that you could not have a more peaceful life.

"Same thing happened to me," Mama continued. "Yet, I wasn't finding out everything. I experienced a sort of relief that I didn't hold back secrets anymore. They were secrets, Sheila, but you did not need all of those questions to stunt your life. "Your father and I chose to keep you safe from harm forevermore. No one could have done that for you except for us. That's how precious you are and your life is to us. We are so very proud of you and your accomplishments."

Mama continued, "Is that lawyer Jonathan Stevenson still around?"

"Yes, Mama," I stated. "He was with me through it all. He stayed here for up until the end of August, and we spent many evenings sitting on my porch way into the night discussing all of my problems and all of Allie's problems."

"You know what happened to Allie's real mother?" Mama questioned.

"Yes, Mama," I answered.

"Well, we don't have time to talk about it," Mama said. "Aren't you leaving for San Jose, California, shortly?"

"Yes, Mama, I'm on my way to see my three best friends from high school," I said.

My Mama and I continued talking for a short period, and after getting all of the luggage into my automobile, I exited my home and continued en route to the airport in Washington, DC.

San Jose

WHEN I ARRIVED and walked through the gates I peered, turning my head from side-to-side as I walked briskly into the entrance of the airport in San Jose. It was packed! I continued walking very briskly until I heard someone yell my name. It was Allie!

I yelled "Allie!"

"Yeah, dear, it's me!"

Following the sound of her voice, I looked forward, and Allie darted out from the carpeted waiting area and ran toward me, clicking her high-heeled shoes against the floor tile. We reached each other with open arms and embraced.

"Oh, dear," Allie stated. "Let me get some tissue. This brings back so many memories—almost like my world has turned upside down. I'm glad I got away from Sommerville. Now I got my grandmamma, Miss Charlotte, and ain't nobody taking her away from me like they cut my mother out of this world. When I think about Sommerville, that town brings back so much pain, dear."

"You look perfect, Allie," I said. "When did you cut your hair? You never cut your hair." Allie stood facing me with almond shaped eyes. She continued to resemble the perfect model after all these years.

"I have been wearing my hair short and tapered for years, Sheila," Allie answered.

"It's perfect," I said.

"Thank you, Sheila," she said. "Mary is set to arrive shortly. I guess we should walk to her gate."

"I guess we should walk to her gate," Valencia imitated. "Mary ain't got any gates up in here."

Allie and I stood still for a few seconds and turned around and spotted Valencia.

"Valencia, are you mocking me?" Allie asked.

"Just playing, Allie." They both hugged.

"This is absolutely wonderful, ladies," I said. "We are going to have the time of our lives."

"How are you managing, Sheila?" Valencia asked.

"I am feeling fine, Val," I said. "Better than ever. I am ready to continue on with my life now that I have everything under control."

"Perfect, because I was worried about what was going on with you, and I didn't know how to help because I live at such a distance," Valencia stated.

A gentle voice came out of nowhere. "I made it." We turned around from our half circle and saw Mary a few steps away from us.

"How is everyone?" Mary said.

"We are doing just fine, Mary," I said. "How are you?"

"It was a wonderful flight, and I am overjoyed at reuniting," Mary said.

"I am so very elated that each of us has the opportunity to reunite," Valencia said. "You traveled from your respective cities across the United States to San Jose, California, on a mission to reacquaint and continue our bond of friendship."

"Anyone interested in the opera tonight?" Valencia asked. "I got four tickets for the seven o'clock show."

About the Author

GLORIA FOSTER HAS had a longstanding desire to publish her writing and has finally accomplished this great feat! She spends most of her time working as a federal government employee. Foster has been involved in work as a paralegal for the United States government for many years, and it also brings her great joy to work as a writer for them. She says this book of fiction is somewhat more enjoyable for her, as it gave her the opportunity to be the maker of her own storyline, characters, and their captivating conversations. She is currently working on a sequel.

Contact the Author

Gloria L. Foster

PO Box 2043

Matteson, IL 60443

Twitter: @GloriaLFoster